Edie
the Garden
Fairy

Special thanks to Narinder Dhami

No part of this publication may be reproduced, stored in a retrieval system, or transmitted in any form or by any means, electronic, mechanical, photocopying, recording, or otherwise, without written permission of the publisher. For information regarding permission, write to Rainbow Magic Limited, c/o HIT Entertainment, 830 South Greenville Avenue, Allen, TX 75002-3320.

ISBN 978-0-545-60526-7

Previously published as Green Fairies #3: *Edie the Garden Fairy* by Orchard U.K. in 2009.

All rights reserved. Published by Scholastic Inc., 557 Broadway, New York, NY 10012, by arrangement with Rainbow Magic Limited.

12 11 10 9 8 7 6 5 4 3 2 1   14 15 16 17 18 19/0

Printed in the U.S.A.   40

This edition first printing, July 2014

Edie
the Garden
Fairy

by Daisy Meadows

SCHOLASTIC INC.

The Earth Fairies must be dreaming
If they think they can escape my scheming.
My goblins are by far the greenest,
And I am definitely the meanest.

Seven fairies out to save the earth?
This very idea fills me with mirth!
I'm sure the world has had enough
Of fairy magic and all that stuff.

So I'm going to steal the fairies' wands
And send them into human lands.
The fairies will think all is lost,
Defeated again—by me, Jack Frost!

Contents

Project Green

"It's another beautiful day, Kirsty!"
Rachel Walker exclaimed happily as she
and her best friend, Kirsty Tate, hurried
along the winding country lane. The
blue sky above them was dotted with
fluffy white clouds, and the sun was
warm on their faces. "Isn't Rainspell
Island just the most *magical* place?"

"I can't think of anywhere I'd rather go on vacation," Kirsty replied, gazing over the lush green fields. The aquamarine sea sparkled in the distance and seagulls wheeled through the crisp, salty air.

The Tates and the Walkers had arrived on the island three days ago to spend the fall break there.

"It's great that we're helping to keep Rainspell clean and beautiful, isn't it, Rachel?" Kirsty added. "Do you have the flyer that came yesterday?"

Rachel pulled the flyer out of her pocket. PROJECT GREEN was written at the top, and underneath it read:

Would YOU like to help the Rainspell Gardening Club make a NEW garden out of an area of unused land? Then please join us at our site on Butterfly Lane tomorrow. Wear old clothes!

"I'm glad we decided to volunteer," Kirsty said as they studied the flyer. "We might have our friends the Earth Fairies to help us with the environment, but we humans have to do our part, too!"

Rachel nodded. Rainspell Island was a very special place because it was where she and Kirsty had first become good friends with the fairies. Since then, the girls had shared many magical, amazing adventures while helping the fairies outwit cold, sly Jack Frost and his goblins.

But now it was Rachel and Kirsty's turn to ask the fairies for help. When the girls had arrived on Rainspell Island, they'd been shocked to see lots of litter scattered across the golden beach. They decided to ask the king and queen of Fairyland to help clean up the human world with fairy magic. King Oberon and Queen Titania had decided that the seven fairies currently in training would become the Earth Fairies. These fairies would help Rachel and Kirsty make the world a greener place. If the Earth Fairies were successful, they would become full-fledged, permanent fairies.

But just as the Fairyland Wand Ceremony was about to begin, the goblins stole the wands that were supposed to be given to the Earth Fairies.

Then Jack Frost's icy spell had immediately sent the goblins and wands spinning into the human world to hide. Jack Frost absolutely refused to help the world become greener, but Rachel and Kirsty were equally determined to make sure all seven of the Earth Fairies got their wands back from the goblins. Then they would work together to make the world become a cleaner, greener place.

"We made a good start," Rachel said cheerfully. "We already tracked down Nicole the Beach Fairy's wand, and Isabella the Air Fairy's, too."

"But it's a little scary to think that there are *five* more goblins running around with fairy wands!" Kirsty frowned. "I hope we find them soon, so the Earth Fairies can get back to work cleaning up our world."

"Remember what Queen Titania said though," Rachel reminded her. "Fairy magic isn't powerful enough to fix all the problems of the environment on its own. Humans have to help, too!"

"I know." Kirsty nodded. "We must be very close to the PROJECT GREEN area now, Rachel," she said, looking around.

The girls kept walking. At the end of

Butterfly Lane they came to a large, empty lot. Rachel and Kirsty could see several people at work. Some were collecting trash that had been dumped and carting it away in wheelbarrows. The girls could see old sofas, rusty bicycles, and broken toys among the junk. Some volunteers were pulling up weeds and digging through the soil. Meanwhile, others were unloading tools and plants from the backs of trucks.

"There's a lot to do," Rachel whispered

to Kirsty. "This doesn't look like a garden at all, yet!"

As the girls drew closer, they saw a woman in overalls carrying a long silver banner that had PROJECT GREEN printed on it in tall emerald-green letters. The woman began trying to hang the banner over a big wooden arch at the entrance of the lot, but it was so long that she got tangled up in it. Rachel and Kirsty rushed to help.

"Oh, thank you!" the woman said breathlessly as the girls helped her. Soon, they had draped the banner over the arch. "Have you come to volunteer?"

The girls nodded
eagerly. "I'm
Rachel and this
is my friend Kirsty,"
Rachel explained.

"Fantastic!"
The woman
smiled at them.
"My name's Janet,
and I'm the head volunteer. It's really
important that we get the garden set up
as soon as possible because"—Janet
glanced anxiously at her watch—"in a
very short time, the builders and their
bulldozers are arriving to turn this space
into a parking lot!"

"That's terrible!" Kirsty gasped.

"We've been learning at school how important green spaces are," Rachel added.

"Yes, we need parks for people to enjoy, not more *parking* lots!" Janet said firmly. "The only person with the power to stop the builders is the mayor of Rainspell Island himself. We explained to the mayor that we want to show him how this space would work well as a garden— and he's promised to come by in an hour to see for himself."

"Only an hour!" Rachel exclaimed. "That doesn't give us much time."

"How can we help?" asked Kirsty.

"See the fields around the vacant lot?" Janet pointed at the fields that bordered the land on two sides. "You can dig holes and plant saplings around the edges of the garden. Then, when the trees have grown, they'll help protect the space from wind and rain. Come on, I'll find some shovels for you."

Rachel and Kirsty followed Janet across the lot. More volunteers were arriving all the time, and there was a buzz of activity as everyone got to work.

"Start over there at the corner of the field, and make sure you space the holes evenly," Janet told the girls as she handed each of them a shovel. "Here are the saplings. We have oak, beech, and ash. If you have any problems, come and find me." With a quick smile, Janet dashed off to welcome a new group of volunteers.

Rachel and Kirsty each collected an armload of tiny saplings and then headed toward the edge of the vacant lot. Suddenly, the saplings in Rachel's  arms began to tremble slightly and tickle her nose. Rachel gasped.

She really wanted to scratch the tip of
her nose, but her arms were full.

"Oh, Kirsty, help!" she called. "The
saplings are tickling my nose. I think I'm
going to sneeze, and then I might drop
everything!"

Kirsty immediately put down her own
saplings and hurried over to Rachel.
Her friend was twitching her nose in a
desperate effort to keep from sneezing.
Quickly, Kirsty took the saplings from
Rachel's arms. She looked closely at the
tiny trees, and then gave a cry of
delight.

"Oh, that's better!" Rachel sighed
with relief, rubbing her nose vigorously.
"But why were the saplings shaking like
that, Kirsty?"

Kirsty laughed. "Try and guess!"

"Is there a spider or a bee hiding in there?" asked Rachel.

"No, but we *have* seen these creatures before, and they have shimmery wings!" Kirsty replied, her eyes twinkling.

"A butterfly?" Rachel guessed. "We *are* on Butterfly Lane, after all."

Kirsty shook her head. She set the saplings on the ground and motioned for Rachel to look more closely. Once again the saplings quivered and trembled—and then a glittery fairy fluttered out of the branches!

Garden Magic!

The fairy hovered in front of Rachel and Kirsty, a huge smile on her face. She wore a pretty blue sun dress, a pink hat, and cute pink rain boots with white polka dots. She carried a straw basket in her hand. "Girls, remember me?" she said. "I'm Edie the Garden Fairy!"

"Hello again, Edie," Rachel said with a laugh.

"If you're here, then that means your wand must be close by!" Kirsty said eagerly.

Edie nodded. "Yes, and I need your help to get it back, girls," she replied.

"As you know, I don't have much magic of my own, because I'm still in training. Getting my wand back will give me a magical boost, and then I'll be able to start taking care of gardens everywhere!"

"We'd love to help, Edie," Kirsty

explained, "but we promised to plant all these saplings."

"We have to make this empty lot look green and beautiful before the mayor arrives, or else it'll be turned into a parking lot!" Rachel added.

Edie looked horrified. "Girls, we can work on the garden *and* look for my wand," she assured them. "Green spaces are *so* important. I'll help you plant the saplings, and we can keep an eye out for the goblin who has my wand at the same time. I just know he's around here somewhere!"

The girls were at the very edge of the

garden, far from the other volunteers.
Edie stayed hidden among the saplings,
just to be on the safe side. Meanwhile,
Kirsty began digging holes, pacing
the distance
between each
one carefully.
Rachel followed
behind her,
planting
the saplings.

"You could
plant them in
groups of three,"
Edie suggested,
peeking out to
watch. "Oak, then beech, then ash, and
so on."

"Good idea," Kirsty agreed, beginning

to dig another hole. "Oh!" She panted. "The ground's really hard here!"

Edie snapped her fingers and a few sparkles of fairy magic drifted down onto the ground. Kirsty tried again, and this time her shovel slid smoothly into the earth.

"Thanks, Edie," she said with a laugh.

Kirsty and Rachel continued planting the saplings around the edge of the garden. Even though they were working hard, they kept an eye out for goblins. But there wasn't any sign of a single one.

"We're almost finished planting these two sides now," Rachel said with satisfaction. She turned and glanced over to where the other volunteers were hard at work. "The garden's starting to look a lot better, isn't it?"

Kirsty nodded. "Look, there's someone handing out cups of water," she said. "Should we get a drink before we finish up here?"

"Yes, and I'm coming, too!" Edie whispered. She fluttered out of the saplings and dived into Rachel's pocket.

The girls walked across the garden, stopping to take a look at the various projects the other volunteers were working on.

"Hi, girls," called Janet, who was planting rows of sweet-scented lavender bushes. "We're making mini-gardens. Come and see!"

Rachel and Kirsty hurried over. One of the mini-gardens was full of herbs planted in circular beds, and another was full of beautiful, fragrant shrubs with pink, white, and purple flowers.

"And that one's a wildflower garden," Janet explained, pointing at the plot next to hers where people were planting poppies, daisies, and cornflowers. "We chose plants that attract wildlife because we want this garden to be a place for people *and* animals to enjoy."

Kirsty turned as a flash of rusty brown caught her eye.

"I think it's working already!" She laughed and pointed across the garden. Rachel, Janet, and the others turned just in time to see a fox dart between the piles of junk. They all grinned.

"This will be a perfect place for foxes and other wildlife!" Edie whispered, popping out of Rachel's pocket. The girls had grabbed their water and were heading back to finish planting the saplings. "Next time we come back to Rainspell

Island, everything will have grown a little more," Kirsty said. "It'll be amazing to know that we helped plant the garden, Rachel!"

"As long as the Gardening Club can convince the mayor to cancel the parking lot," Rachel reminded her friend with a sigh. Suddenly, she gasped in horror. "Kirsty, look at our saplings!"

Kirsty cried out in surprise as she stared at the tiny trees they'd planted. Half the saplings had been pulled from the earth. They were now laying limply on the ground!

"What happened?" Rachel wondered. Kirsty shook here head. All their hard work was ruined!

Goblin Gardener

Rachel knelt down and picked up one of the saplings.

"Maybe the mini-gardens are working too well already!" she suggested. "An animal might have come along and dug them up."

"Maybe," Edie agreed. "But they have to be replanted quickly, or they'll die."

She took a quick glance around, and
then snapped her fingers. A faint mist of
fairy dust surrounded
the saplings.
When it
cleared, the
girls were
relieved to see
that they were
all neatly planted in the holes
again.

"Thanks, Edie," they said in chorus.

"Oh, no!" someone yelled behind
them.

Edie quickly hid in Rachel's pocket
again. The girls spun around, hearts
pounding, as they heard other shouts
of amazement. Had someone spotted
the tiny fairy?

Janet was looking upset, so the girls rushed over to her.

"What happened, Janet?" Rachel asked.

"Everything's going wrong!" Janet sighed. "Someone has uprooted one of the big butterfly bushes we planted *and* knocked a big bag of flower seeds on the ground!"

In the middle of the garden, Rachel and Kirsty could see a big shrub with

purple flowers lying on its side, its roots in the air next to a pile of tiny brown seeds. An old broken chair and a couple of rusty tools lay close by.

"And someone's moving all the junk around, too!" Janet rubbed her forehead in frustration. "Those things were in the trash pile, and now they're back in the garden! At this rate we'll never be finished in time for the mayor's visit!"

"We can't let that happen, Rachel," Kirsty whispered to her friend.

"We'll have to work much faster, everyone," Janet called. "Otherwise all our hard work will be paved over and our plants will be replaced with parked cars!"

"If only I could find my wand," Edie

said as everyone got back to work. "Then I could help finish the garden with fairy magic."

Rachel frowned. "Where there's mess and trouble and a missing wand, there must be a goblin!" she pointed out.

"Let's find him before he causes any more damage," Kirsty suggested.

She quickly climbed up onto the back of a nearby truck. "Come on, Rachel, we can get a good view of the garden from here!"

Rachel climbed up, too, and the girls looked carefully around the garden. All the volunteers were back at work again, and they couldn't see anything out of the ordinary.

Then Kirsty clutched Rachel's arm.

"Look!" she whispered. "Over there on the edge of the garden, by the biggest garbage pile!"

Rachel saw a very short person wearing a big,

floppy straw hat and oversize overalls. He was sorting through the pile of junk and throwing bits of trash right and left, making a mess of the tidy pile.

"Come on!" Rachel murmured, climbing down from the truck.

The girls ran across the garden. As they got closer to the strange-looking gardener, they noticed his big feet and large, pointy ears.

"It's a goblin!" Kirsty said, eyes wide.

Ribbon of Sparkles

"Hurry, girls!" Edie urged them.

Rachel and Kirsty dashed up to the goblin. Luckily, he was standing pretty far away from the other volunteers, and no one had noticed him.

"Where's Edie's wand?" Rachel demanded as she and Kirsty cornered the goblin. "We'd like it back, please!"

The goblin shrieked in surprise. Then he scowled fiercely as Edie fluttered out of Rachel's pocket.

"Pesky girls!" he muttered. "And a pesky fairy, too. Well, I wouldn't give you the wand, even if I had it."

"What do you mean?" Kirsty asked.

The goblin shrugged. "I lost it in all the mess I made!" he muttered sheepishly.

The girls and Edie glanced at one another in dismay.

"The wand could be *anywhere!*" Kirsty groaned.

"Why are you trying to undo all our good work?" Rachel asked the goblin.

"This place is supposed to be green, isn't it?" the goblin asked. "And considering I'm the only thing that's *truly* green around here, I get to decide what goes on!" He folded his arms and stared stubbornly at Edie and the girls. "And I like the sound of a nice, smooth parking lot where I'll be able to roller-skate!"

Edie sighed. "My wand changes itself to fit the person who used it last, so it'll be goblin-size now," she told the girls. "That means it will be easier to spot. But we have to find it quickly before it falls into human hands. I don't know *what* will happen then!"

"I'm going to find the wand first!" the goblin insisted, and he began pulling the junk pile apart. "I know I saw it when I was scattering the trash around the garden," the goblin mumbled to himself, picking up a battered old radio. He pushed a button, and music began to play.

The goblin looked puzzled. "Why was this thrown away?" he asked.

"I don't know why people can't put their trash where it belongs, and not dump it in the countryside," Rachel said.

"They could even have recycled some of this," Kirsty added.

The goblin began burrowing into the pile again, tossing pieces of junk everywhere. Edie and the girls glared at him.

"We'd better start looking through the other garbage piles," Rachel whispered to her friends. "We have to find the wand before the goblin does!"

Edie, Rachel, and Kirsty moved to a nearby trash pile and began searching through the rusty tools, old TV sets, and broken bicycles. As Kirsty picked up a crumpled cardboard box, she once again noticed a flash of rusty brown from the corner of her eye.

The fox is back, she thought, turning to look.

Kirsty saw the fox dart toward one of the nearby fields. She blinked. It looked like the fox was leaving behind a ribbon of sparkles as he ran.

"Look!" Kirsty said, pointing out the fox to Rachel and Edie. "Isn't that odd?"

Edie gasped with surprise. "That fox has my wand!" she exclaimed. "He's leaving a trail of fairy magic!" She turned to Rachel and Kirsty. "It'll be faster if we fly after him, girls—and I have just enough magic of my own to turn you into fairies!"

Edie hovered above Rachel and Kirsty and clapped her hands. A shower of glittering fairy dust floated down onto the girls,

and they began to shrink. Meanwhile,
shimmering fairy wings appeared on
their shoulders.

"Quick, we can't let it get away!" Edie
whispered, so that the goblin couldn't
hear.

The three friends rose into the air and
flew after the fox, who was now
bounding across the field.

"Don't lose sight of him!" Kirsty
panted as they zoomed through the air.

Rachel glanced down and cried in
dismay. "The goblin's following us!" she
called. "He figured out that we know
where the wand is!"

Which Wand?

"I think the fox has realized that we're following him, too!" Kirsty shouted, as the fox cleverly ducked into a clump of tall grass, out of sight.

"Don't be scared, Mr. Fox," Edie called as the fox reappeared deeper in the field and then bolted off again. "We won't hurt you!"

The fox slowed down a little and glanced up at Edie and the girls, waving his bushy tail to and fro. They could see he had Edie's wand clutched between his teeth.

The goblin dashed across the field. "Interfering fairies!" he screeched furiously. "Give me back my wand!"

The fox looked very nervous and took off again. He ran right into the middle of a tall bush and disappeared.

"The goblin scared him away!" Kirsty groaned.

"Where's the wand?" the goblin
demanded suspiciously, staring up at the
three fairies as they hovered over the
bush. "Is it in here?"

The goblin began shoving the branches
of the bush aside. Suddenly, the fox
poked his furry head out. The goblin
shrieked with glee when he saw the
glittering wand.

"Give that to me!" he shouted, trying
to grab it from the fox.

But the fox was too quick for him.
He jumped out of the bush and ran
off. The goblin lunged after him but
only managed to grab the fox's tail.

The stubborn goblin held on. The fox
finally wriggled free, throwing the
goblin off-balance.

"Help!" the goblin screeched as he fell

backward into the
bush. He tried to
pull himself out,
but he got tangled
up in his extra-
large overalls.
Edie and the girls
couldn't help laughing.

"There's the fox," Rachel whispered.
The fox had stopped a little way off
and was staring at the goblin, Edie,
Rachel, and Kirsty with curiosity. He
still had the wand in his mouth.

"If we try to catch the fox, he'll just
run off again," Edie said in a low voice.

"We have to persuade him to give us
the wand."

"We'd better get rid of the goblin
first!" Kirsty pointed out. She glanced at
the goblin, who was still struggling to
untangle himself. "He just keeps scaring
the fox away."

"I have an idea!" Edie winked at
them. Then she waved her arms in a
pretty pattern and a few sparkles of fairy
magic appeared. They floated on the
breeze across the
field. One
landed on the
grass, and Rachel
and Kirsty were
amazed to see
two rabbits
pop their heads

out of a hole at that very spot. Another couple of sparkles settled on a nearby tree. The next moment, two squirrels appeared out of the leaves.

"Thank you for answering our call for help, my friends!" Edie said, as the squirrels and rabbits gathered around them. "Can you distract that goblin while I use my magic to talk to the fox?"

The rabbits and the squirrels looked at the goblin, who was still trying to untangle himself.

The squirrels looked puzzled.

Rachel frowned. She stared down at the long blades of grass around them, and she suddenly had an idea.

"Quick, Edie, make me and Kirsty human-size again, please!" Rachel said.

Edie nodded and did so.

"Now, Kirsty, help me break off four blades of grass the same size as Edie's wand," Rachel instructed.

"Oh, I think I can guess what your idea is, Rachel!" Kirsty laughed as she selected a tall blade of grass.

The girls chose four grass stalks in all. Then they opened the magic lockets Queen Titania had given them and  sprinkled the grass with fairy dust. Now the blades of grass shimmered in the sun just like Edie's wand.

"Fake wands!" Edie said with a smile, as the girls handed a blade of grass to each of the rabbits and the squirrels. "What a brilliant idea."

"Now run off in different directions!"
Kirsty whispered to the rabbits and
squirrels. They all nodded and then
scurried away.

By now, the goblin had finally
scrambled to his feet.

"Look!" Rachel shouted, pointing
across the field. "I see the wand!"

"Yes, a squirrel has it!"
Kirsty added.

The goblin stopped
and glanced around
while Kirsty,
Rachel, and Edie
held their breath.
Would the
fake wands
fool the
goblin?

Rainbow Park!

"Ah!" the goblin jeered, sticking his tongue out at them. "You can't trick *me*!"

He pointed in the opposite direction where a rabbit was hopping along, trailing glitter. "That rabbit has the wand!" the goblin yelled. And he chased after it.

"Now we can talk to the fox in peace!" Edie whispered.

The girls walked quietly over to the fox. Edie hovered above them. This time the fox didn't run away.

"Hello," Kirsty said softly. "That wand belongs to our friend Edie the Garden Fairy, and she'd really like it back."

The fox looked stubborn.

"If Edie gets her wand back, we'll be able to finish the garden," Rachel explained. "If we don't finish, it'll be turned into a parking lot instead."

"There won't be any flowers or trees,"

58

Kirsty added. "Just lots and lots of concrete and cement."

The fox seemed to frown. He sat there for a moment, and then he placed the wand on the grass. He stepped back.

"Oh, thank you!" Edie exclaimed joyfully. She fluttered down and touched the wand, which immediately shrank down to fairy-size.

The fox smiled and bounded away.

Rachel turned as she heard a loud, rumbling sound in the distance. "Here come the bulldozers!" she gasped. "That means the mayor must have arrived, too."

Edie and the girls hurried back to
the garden. As they went, they saw
the rabbits and the squirrels
crisscrossing the field in
front of
the goblin,
waving
their
fake wands.
The goblin
was chasing first
one, then another,
looking very frustrated.

"I wonder when he'll realize that the
animals have pretend wands?" Rachel
laughed.

"I'll send him home soon if he doesn't
figure it out!" Edie replied with a wink.

As the girls reached the garden, the bulldozers pulled up to the lot. All the volunteers, including Janet, were gathered around the mayor, near the wooden arch. But Rachel and Kirsty were disappointed to see that the garden hadn't been finished.

"Don't worry, girls," Edie whispered, ducking out of sight behind Kirsty's hair. "Now that I have my wand, I can help!"

Rachel and Kirsty watched eagerly as Edie waved her wand. A mist of glittering fairy dust cleared away all the trash in a flash. Another flick of Edie's wand made the flowers bloom just a little more brightly and it also made all the green leaves shine. Then Edie sent a stream of magic sparkles toward the middle of the garden and a large bed of beautiful flowers appeared in a rainbow of colors.

"Please come and see what we've done," Janet said to the mayor, as everyone turned to look at the garden. "We didn't have much time, but—" She stopped, looking surprised. "Well, it looks even more beautiful than I thought it did!"

"This is just wonderful!" the mayor declared, his face breaking into a smile. "Please show me around, Janet."

"You and all the other volunteers have done a great job," Edie whispered to Kirsty and Rachel, as Janet took the mayor on a tour of the garden. "Now that I have my wand I'm going to take care of all the gardens on Rainspell, and everywhere else!"

"I don't think we need a parking lot here," the mayor announced with a smile. "I think that this space should definitely be a wildlife garden!"

Rachel and Kirsty cheered and applauded with everyone else as the bulldozers rumbled away. Edie looked delighted, too.

"I need to get back to Fairyland and tell everyone the good news," she murmured. "Thank you, girls, and remember to keep a lookout for goblins and wands!" Edie blew them both a kiss and disappeared in a cloud of fairy dust.

"Doesn't it feel good to do something for Rainspell Island, Rachel?" Kirsty said happily. "After all, this is where we met our very first magic friends, the Rainbow Fairies!"

Rachel nodded in agreement.

"What should we call the park?" the mayor asked Janet.

Janet glanced at the cluster of colorful flowers in the middle. "How about Rainbow Park?" she suggested.

Rachel and Kirsty glanced at each other with a smile as everyone cheered.

"Perfect!" Rachel whispered.

Rachel and Kirsty found Nicole, Isabella,
and Edie's missing magic words.
Now it's time for them to help

Coral

the Reef Fairy!

Join their next adventure
in this special sneak peek. . . .

Magical Sparkles

Kirsty Tate grinned as she stepped onto the beach. "This looks *fun*!" she exclaimed, gazing around in excitement.

Her best friend, Rachel Walker, was close behind. "And there's so much to do," she said, her eyes bright. "Where should we go first?"

The two girls had come with their

parents to Rainspell Beach, where the local surfing club was holding a "Save the Coral Reefs" event. As Kirsty and Rachel looked around, they could see a crowd of people dancing to the lively beat of a samba band, a line of food stands that all smelled delicious, and an information center surrounded by flags displaying pictures of bright, colorful tropical fish.

"Maybe we should split up and meet back here in an hour for lunch?" Mr. Walker, Rachel's dad, suggested.

"Good idea," Rachel replied. "How about we meet you at the information center at twelve?" She slipped an arm through Kirsty's. "Come on, let's explore."

The girls made their way into the

crowd, enjoying the hustle and bustle of the event. They were on Rainspell Island for a school break. So far they'd had a very exciting few days helping their new fairy friends, the Earth Fairies.

"There's another good reason for going off on our own," Kirsty said, thinking about the adventures they'd had lately. "We might meet another fairy today."

Rachel grinned and crossed her fingers. "Here's hoping!" she said.

At the start of the week, Kirsty and Rachel had magically transported themselves to Fairyland to ask King Oberon and Queen Titania for their help in cleaning up the human world. The girls had met seven fairies-in-training who each had a special mission. When their training was complete, they would become the Earth Fairies. Their jobs would be to help save the environment in both the human world and in Fairyland. But before the fairies had received their wands and could start work, Jack Frost had appeared. He'd declared his goblins were the only truly "green" creatures and had ordered them to steal the magic wands and hide them in the human world!

RAINBOW magic™

Which Magical Fairies Have You Met?

- ❑ The Rainbow Fairies
- ❑ The Weather Fairies
- ❑ The Jewel Fairies
- ❑ The Pet Fairies
- ❑ The Dance Fairies
- ❑ The Music Fairies
- ❑ The Sports Fairies
- ❑ The Party Fairies
- ❑ The Ocean Fairies
- ❑ The Night Fairies
- ❑ The Magical Animal Fairies
- ❑ The Princess Fairies
- ❑ The Superstar Fairies
- ❑ The Fashion Fairies
- ❑ The Sugar & Spice Fairies

RAINBOW magic™

SPECIAL EDITION

Which Magical Fairies Have You Met?

3 stories in each one!

- ☐ Joy the Summer Vacation Fairy
- ☐ Holly the Christmas Fairy
- ☐ Kylie the Carnival Fairy
- ☐ Stella the Star Fairy
- ☐ Shannon the Ocean Fairy
- ☐ Trixie the Halloween Fairy
- ☐ Gabriella the Snow Kingdom Fairy
- ☐ Juliet the Valentine Fairy
- ☐ Mia the Bridesmaid Fairy
- ☐ Flora the Dress-Up Fairy
- ☐ Paige the Christmas Play Fairy
- ☐ Emma the Easter Fairy
- ☐ Cara the Camp Fairy
- ☐ Destiny the Rock Star Fairy
- ☐ Belle the Birthday Fairy
- ☐ Olympia the Games Fairy
- ☐ Selena the Sleepover Fairy
- ☐ Cheryl the Christmas Tree Fairy
- ☐ Florence the Friendship Fairy
- ☐ Lindsay the Luck Fairy
- ☐ Brianna the Tooth Fairy
- ☐ Autumn the Falling Leaves Fairy
- ☐ Keira the Movie Star Fairy
- ☐ Addison the April Fool's Day Fairy

■ SCHOLASTIC

Find all of your favorite fairy friends at
scholastic.com/rainbowmagic

HIT entertainment

RMSPECIAL12